A Bit of Dancing

Helen Oxenbury

WALKER BOOKS
AND SUBSIDIARIES
LONDON · BOSTON · SYDNEY

Class No. _O-4_ Acc No. C/107 253

Author: Oxenbury: H Loc:

1. **This book may be kept three weeks. It is to be
   ret~~** J(O4) C/107253 **last date stamped below.**
   Holen **ged for every week or part
   le.** (Code 23)

12 OCT 2016		
28 JUL 2017		

For Dreas

The Dancing Class and
Playschool first published 1983
The Visitor first published 1984
by Walker Books Ltd
87 Vauxhall Walk
London SE11 5HJ

This edition published 1995

2 4 6 8 10 9 7 5 3 1

© 1983, 1984 Helen Oxenbury

This book has been typeset in Goudy.

Printed in Hong Kong

British Library Cataloguing in Publication Data
A catalogue record for this book is available from the British Library.

ISBN 0-7445-3778-9 (hb)
ISBN 0-7445-3723-1 (pb)

The Dancing Class

Mum said I should go to dancing classes.

8

"We'll take these tights.
She'll soon grow into them."

"We'll just make your hair tidy
like the others'."

"Heads up, tummies in,
knees straight and point
your toes," the teacher said.

"Don't cry, you'll soon learn.
I'll show you the right way
to tie up your shoes."

"You danced very well," the teacher told me. "Will you come again next week?"

"This is what we do, Mum.
Watch. I'll do the gallop
all the way home."

Playschool

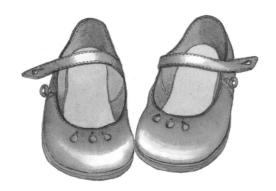

"Up you get! You mustn't be late
for your first day at playschool.
And you can wear your new shoes."

"Don't be shy, you'll make lots
of new friends," Mum said.
"I don't think I'm going to like it,"
I whispered.

"Don't leave me, Mum!"
"It's all right,"
  the teacher said.
"Your mummy can
  stay for a bit,
  if you like."

"This is Nara!
  She's just hurt
  her knee."

"Look! You've got the same shoes on."

"I'm just popping out to the shops for a moment," said Mum.

"Come on, you two," the teacher said.
"We can all pretend to
 be animals."

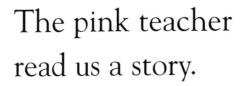

The pink teacher
read us a story.

We had our
elevenses,
and Nara
and I
shared.

"When you've all been to the
lavatory and washed your hands,
then we'll sing some songs."

"Off you go!
Your mums and dads are waiting.
See you all at school tomorrow!"

The Visitor

Mum was expecting Mr Thorpney.
They were going to talk about work.
"You'll have to be good and amuse
yourself while he's here," she said.

35

"Come in and sit down," Mum said.
"I'll make you some coffee."
"Will you remove the cat?"
Mr Thorpney asked. "Cats
make me sneeze."

"Shouldn't you be at school?"
Mr Thorpney asked.
"I'm not big enough," I said. "How
long are you staying?"
Mum came in with the coffee.
"Mr Thorpney doesn't
like our cat," I said.

"Please put the cat
out now," Mum said.
"We must get on with
our work."

I let them talk
for ages.
Then I turned on
the radio and did
a bit of dancing.

"Please do that somewhere else," Mum said.

41

I felt hot, so I opened the window.

"Oh no!" said Mum. "You've let the cat back in!"

Mr Thorpney
sneezed.

"Look, Mum," I said. "Mr Thorpney
has spilled his coffee."

43

"Oh dear," said Mum,
    after Mr Thorpney had gone.
"He's forgotten his hat."